Too Much NOISE In The Library

Susan Margaret Chapman

Illustrated by
Abby Carter

UpstartBooks™

Janesville, Wisconsin
www.upstartbooks.com

*For the Milliken Mills Public School
Library. Thanks to Rebecca Upjohn,
Laurel Dee Gugler, Jill Pearson, Tiffany
Stone, Thereza Dos Santos, Michael
Kats, and especially Ken McRoberts.*
—S. M. C.

For Doug, Samantha and Carter
—A. C.

Published by UpstartBooks
401 S. Wright Road
P.O. Box 5207
Janesville, Wisconsin 53547-5207
1-800-448-4887

Text © 2010 by Susan Margaret Chapman
Illustrations © 2010 by Abby Carter

Not long ago there was a busy school librarian.
Her name was Ms. Reade, and she ran a lively,
booming media center.

Every day
the book returns thumped,
kerplop kerplop,

the computer keys tapped, **clickety click**,

the printers screeched,
zippedy zing,

the DVDs
blared,
**blabbety
blab**,

the pages turned, **rustle rustle**,

the
teachers
chattered,

yackety yack,

the children giggled,
hee hee, hee hee,

and
Adam asked a million
questions.

One day, the mayor of the town happened to be visiting the school. He stopped at the open library doors and peeked in.

"I love libraries!" said the mayor. "They're so peaceful and quiet." So he walked in.

Ms. Reade was
working at her desk.
All the children were
out for recess.
The mayor looked
around happily.
It was peaceful and quiet.

Ms. Reade stood up in surprise and said,
"Why, welcome to the library, Mr. Mayor.
Please come in and have a look around."
The mayor thanked her politely and started
to browse through the dinosaur section.

Suddenly, the bell rang.
Recess was over. Children
and teachers poured
through the library doors.

Ms. Reade was piling some books and CDs and puppets on a cart. "Mr. Mayor," she said, "I'm just taking these things down to the kindergarten. I'll be right back. Please make yourself at home."
And he did.

But

the book returns thumped, **kerplop kerplop**,
the computer keys tapped, **clickety click**,
the printers screeched, **zippedy zing**,
the DVDs blared, **blabbety blab**,
the pages turned, **rustle rustle**,
the teachers chattered, **yackety yack**.
the children giggled, **hee hee, hee hee**,

and Adam asked a
million questions.

The mayor frowned a very big frown. He stood in the middle of the library. He covered his ears. Finally he bellowed,

"THERE'S TOO MUCH NOISE IN THE LIBRARY! SOMETHING MUST BE DONE ABOUT THIS!"

They all stopped.
They looked at the mayor.

Shaneera put down her pencil and said, "Why don't you try closing the book return box, Mr. Mayor?"

"Hmmmm…" said the mayor. "Good idea!" And he did.

Now no books thumped,

kerplop
kerplop.

But the computer keys tapped, **clickety click**,
the printers screeched, **zippedy zing**,
the DVDs blared, **blabbety blab**,
the pages turned, **rustle rustle**,

the teachers chattered,
yackety yack.

the children giggled,
hee hee, hee hee,

and Adam
asked a
million
questions.

"It is still too noisy! What can we do?" grumbled the mayor.

And Zareb said, "Maybe you should turn off the computers and printers, Mr. Mayor."

"Hmmmm..." said the mayor.

"Good idea!" And he did.

Now no computer keys tapped, **clickety click** and no printers screeched, **zippedy zing**.

But the DVDs blared, **blabbety blab,**

the pages turned, **rustle rustle,**

the teachers chattered, **yackety yack,**

the children giggled, **hee hee, hee hee,**

and Adam asked
a million questions.

"STILL too noisy," said the mayor.

"Turn off the DVD players then, Mr. Mayor," said Emily.

"Hmmmm..." said the mayor. "Good idea!"

And he did.

Now, no DVDs blared **blabbety blab.**

But the pages turned, **rustle rustle,** the teachers chattered, **yackety yack,** the children giggled, **hee hee, hee hee,** and Adam asked a million questions.

"Noisy!" said the mayor.

"Maybe you should lock up all the books,"
said Maria.

"Hmmmm..." said the mayor. "Good idea!" And he did.

Now, no pages turned **rustle rustle**.

But the teachers chattered, **yackety yack**,

the children giggled, **hee hee, hee hee**,

and Adam asked
a million questions.

"STILL noisy," said the mayor.

"How about
telling the teachers
to go for coffee?"
said Daniel.

"Hmmmm..." said the mayor.
"Good idea!" And he did.

Now, no teachers chattered, **yackety yack.**

But the children giggled, **hee hee, hee hee,**

and Adam
asked a
million
questions.

"STILL too noisy," said the mayor.

"Why don't you send all the children back to class, Mr. Mayor?" said Adam.

"Hmmmm..." said the mayor. "Good idea!" So he did.

Even Adam.

Suddenly it was VERY QUIET.

"How peaceful!" said the mayor, as he sat in the rocking chair and looked around. He rocked back and forth. He read a dinosaur book. Then he read another one.

He started tapping his fingers. He twiddled his thumbs. He got up and walked across the library. Finally, he went back to the rocking chair and had a nap.

Ms. Reade came
bustling in the door.
She stopped in shock.

"Mr. Mayor," she said.
"What has happened to
the library?!"

"Well," said the mayor
with a superior smile,
"the library
was just
too noisy.

The book returns thumped,
kerplop kerplop, so I closed the box.

The computer keys tapped, **clickety click**,

the printers screeched, **zippedy zing**,

and the DVDs blared, **blabbety blab**,
so I turned them all off.

The pages turned, **rustle rustle**,
so I locked up all the books.

The teachers chattered, **yackety yack**,
so I told them to go for coffee.

The children giggled,
hee hee, hee hee,
so I sent them back to class.

Especially Adam and his
million questions."

Ms. Reade raised her left eyebrow. She tapped her foot. She folded her arms. She didn't know what to say. After all, he WAS the mayor. She thought for a minute. Finally she said, "Mr. Mayor, do you really LIKE the library like this?"

The mayor looked around the library. He felt a yawn coming on. "Maybe it IS a bit TOO quiet," he said.

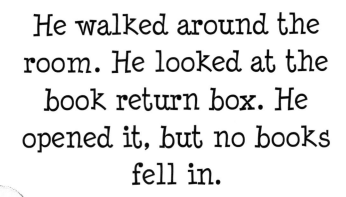

He walked around the room. He looked at the book return box. He opened it, but no books fell in.

He walked around the room again. He looked at the computers and printers.

He turned them on, but they stayed quiet and still.

He walked around the room again. He looked at the DVD players. He put on his favorite fairy tale. It was still too quiet.

He walked around the room again. He looked at the locked shelves. He unlocked all the books, but they sat silently on the shelf.

"It is STILL too quiet," said the mayor. He scratched his head. "What shall we do?"

"Well, Mr. Mayor, there is still something missing," said Ms. Reade.

The mayor walked VERY, VERY slowly around the room. He saw some students peeking through a window. He saw a teacher peering through a crack in the door. He looked at the empty chairs.

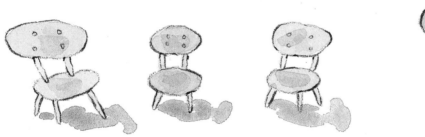

Ms. Reade raised both eyebrows.

The mayor stopped. He grinned.

"Let's ask the teachers to bring back the children!" he said.

"HMMMM..." said Ms. Reade. "GOOD IDEA!" So they did.

AND THEN...

the book returns thumped,
kerplop kerplop,

the computer keys tapped,
clickety click,

the printers screeched, **zippedy zing,**

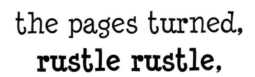

the DVDs blared,
blabbety blab,

the pages turned,
rustle rustle,

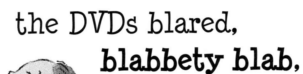

the teachers chattered,
yackety yack,

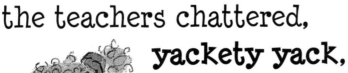

the children giggled,
hee hee, hee hee,

and Adam asked
a million questions.

The mayor listened to the buzz and bustle around him.

"I love libraries," he said.

"They're so busy and lively!"

Ms. Reade smiled a quiet smile,

and she started to answer Adam's questions.